Ballerina!

Ballerina!

by Peter Sís

SCHOLASTIC INC.

New York Toronto London Auckland Sydney
Mexico City New Delhi Hong Kong Buenos Aires

ISBN 0-439-45110-8

12 11 10 9 8 7 6 5 4 3 2 1   2 3 4 5 6 7/0

Printed in the U.S.A.   23

First Scholastic printing, September 2002

Black line art is combined with watercolors for the full-color illustrations.
The text type is Bitstream Swiss 721.

For my niece Tereza Sís

**Terry loves
ballet.**

She can't
wait to dance.

**She puts on her tights
to warm up.**

STRETCH

She puts on her
pink tutu and dances
The Nutcracker.

TWIRL

She puts on her
red leotard and dances
a fire dance.

LEAP

She puts on her
blue gown and dances
The Sleeping Beauty.

TiPTOE

She puts on her
yellow turban and
dances a tiger dance.

REACH

She puts on her
white feather boa and
dances *Swan Lake.*

DIP

She puts on her
green hat and dances
a spring dance.

FLUTTER

She puts on her
violet cape and
dances *Cinderella*.

FLOAT

She puts on her green, blue, violet, red, pink, yellow, and white scarves—

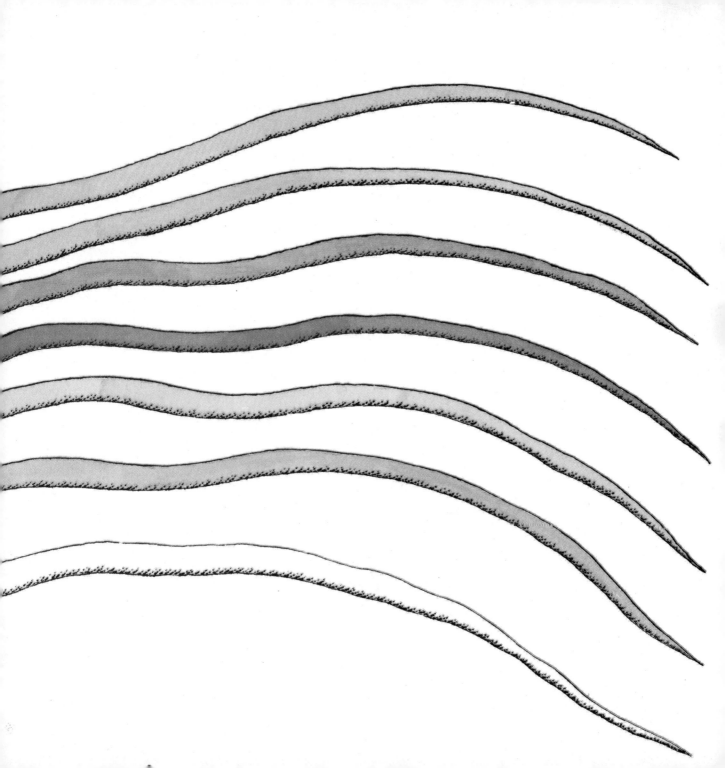

and is the best ballerina of all.

Her audience claps and claps and claps.